Pinocchio

LANDOLL

There was once an old **carpenter** called Gepetto who was very lonely. One day he decided to make a **puppet** to keep him company. He took a block of **wood** and began to shape the head with his **knife**. Very soon the puppet was finished.

carpenter

puppet

wood

knife

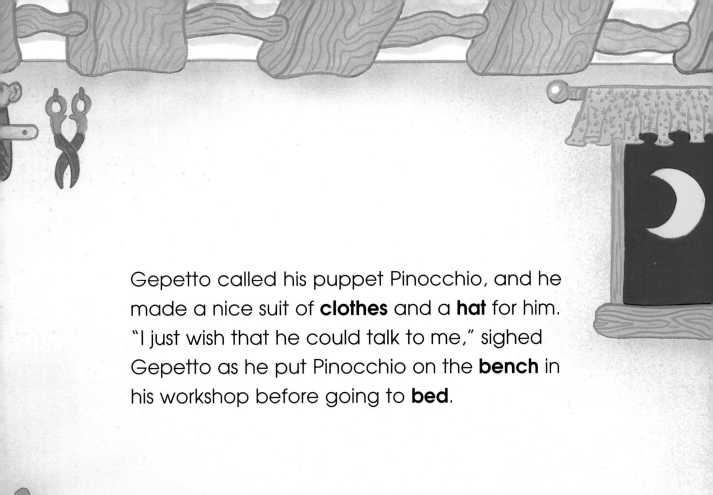

Gepetto called his puppet Pinocchio, and he made a nice suit of **clothes** and a **hat** for him. "I just wish that he could talk to me," sighed Gepetto as he put Pinocchio on the **bench** in his workshop before going to **bed**.

clothes

hat

bench

bed

However, later that night a **fairy** visited the **workshop** and brought Pinocchio to life by waving her magic **wand**.
The next morning Gepetto was delighted to find that Pinocchio could walk and talk like any other boy. "You must go to **school**," Gepetto told Pinocchio.

fairy

workshop

wand

school,"

But the carpenter was so poor that he had to sell his **coat** to buy the **books** that Pinocchio would need for his studies.

On his way to school for the first time, Pinocchio saw a **circus** and he wanted to go inside to watch the **performance**.

coat

books

circus

performance

Pinocchio sold his school books to a **boy** to get enough **money** for his **ticket** into the circus. Once inside, he began chatting to the **fire-eater** who said that Pinocchio could stay and work in the circus. "I can't" Pinocchio replied. "My father is poor and he needs me."

boy

money

ticket

fire-eater

The fire-eater was kind-hearted so he gave Pinocchio some coins and sent him on his way. Unhappily, on his way **home** Pinocchio met a **cat** and a **fox**. They were very cunning and robbed Pinocchio of his money. He tried to catch them as they ran off but he tripped and grazed his **knee**.

home

cat

fox

knee

Unknown to Pinocchio, his friend, the fairy, was watching over him so she asked him what had happened.

"A **monster** with big **ears** attacked me," he replied, and immediately his **nose** grew to an enormous length.

"It will do that every time you tell a lie," warned the fairy with a **smile**.

monster

ears

nose

smile

"Where is my father?" Pinocchio asked the fairy.

"He went across the **sea** to find you when you did not return from school," she said.

"I must go after him," said Pinocchio. He ran to the **pier**, took off his **shoes** and jumped into the sea, but was swallowed up by a huge **whale**. What a surprise Pinocchio got, for the same whale had also swallowed Gepetto.

sea
pier
shoes
whale

Pinocchio tickled the whale's inside with a **fishing hook** which it had swallowed, and this made the whale sneeze. When the whale, sneezed Pinocchio and Gepetto flew out of its **mouth**. Their friend the fairy rescued them from the water in a **boat,** and Pinocchio was so pleased to be free that he promised his father that he would never be naughty again.

Pinocchio

fishing hook

mouth

boat

These are some of the words that you have read in the story of Pinocchio. Can you find them?

carpenter	coat	monster
puppet	books	ears
wood	circus	nose
knife	performance	smile
clothes	boy	sea
hat	money	pier
bench	ticket	shoes
bed	fire-eater	whale
fairy	home	Pinocchio
workshop	cat	fishing hook
wand	fox	mouth
school	knee	boat